DEDICATED TO:

SPECIAL MESSAGE:

Made in United States
North Haven, CT
28 September 2022

24642731R00057